RESCUED BY THE MOUNTAIN MAN

MIA BRODY

1
PIPER

"Can you come here for a minute?" Brock asks as he stands in the doorway of his office. My big brother is the sheriff here in South Tahoe. He's also my boss though I don't think of him that way.

For years, my dad was the sheriff. He proudly served the people of South Tahoe. When Brock followed in his steps and went to the police academy, he couldn't have been prouder. Except that Brock didn't come home right away. He spent years as a homicide detective until my dad's sudden passing brought him home. He assumed my father's old post and life has continued on.

I step into the cream-colored office that I updated for my father about a year before he died. He encouraged me to go after my dreams, but I could never imagine working anywhere else. So, I went to school and became a dispatcher.

Even before that, I was spending every spare minute at the station. I loved being around my dad. He always doted on me and there are still moments when I can't believe he's gone. It seems like a dream that I keep waiting to wake up from.

"What's up?" I spot the pastry on the desk. I bounce over to it. This one is my favorite, the cheesecake Danish with extra filling and glaze on top. I sniff the coffee, confirming that it's a salted caramel mocha from Patty's Cakes, a local bakery here in town.

"Big brother wants a favor." I take a seat across from his desk. He doesn't have to butter me up. He only has to ask, and I'll do anything I can to help him. But that's not going to stop me from eating my treat.

He takes his seat across from me and watches me bite into the pastry. I know that look on his face. It's the one he gets when he's about to tell me something I don't want to hear. "The county has me personally reviewing the personnel records and making sure everything is updated."

I nod along. Since Brock took over, the county is making us upgrade to digital records for everything.

Dad fought them for years but with him no longer here, the task of dragging the station into the twenty-first century has fallen on my brother's shoulders. "Do you need help with the personnel files?"

I might be a dispatcher, but I'll do anything to keep my dad's legacy running. From getting coffee to sweeping the floors, there's never been a task I wouldn't do here.

My dad always believed that the highest form of leadership was servanthood and he instilled in me from a young age that the police and other first responders are servants of the people. Maybe that's why I've had such a hard time admitting that I've been dreaming a new dream. It's quiet, tucked away in a corner of my heart.

"There's a problem with your file," he says.

"You mean with uploading it to the new system?" The salted caramel taste hits my tongue perfectly. Autumn is just around the corner, my favorite time of year.

"No, with your file. What I'm seeing says you've never taken a day off since you started as a volunteer at sixteen. You even came in on the day of dad's funeral."

"He would have wanted me to carry on," I

counter, keeping my voice even. If there's one thing I've learned about working in an office full of men, it's to keep my emotions in check. Getting angry or upset only feeds into the idea that women aren't suited for some workplace environments. Fortunately, my brother doesn't carry any of these sexist ideas.

Brock studies me as if he's seeing me for the first time. Maybe he is. After all, we're ten years apart in age. "The county owes you a lot of vacation days, and it's time you took them."

I finish the rest of the Danish and brush crumbs from my pants. "No, I'm good. I'm not going to crack up on you."

My brother saw some gritty things as a homicide detective. He may not have said it all those years ago, but he was really struggling. It was why I got him into reading romance books. Something with a guaranteed happy ending can be a source of hope when life doesn't make sense anymore. My brother even found a romance author and fell in love with her. It doesn't get any cuter than that.

Because of his own struggles, Brock is pushing for more training and education about mental health for first responders. It's slow going but he's trying to raise the funding the county would need for his program.

There's a knock on the door then Zoey pokes her head through. She's Brock's wife and the romance author I mentioned. She writes books about adorkable plus-size heroines who fall for strong alpha males. She's pretty much my hero and the reason I've started writing my own books. They're not very good but Zoey says to keep going. "Hey, Pipe! I'm glad you're here! I wanted to talk to you about the lodge."

I don't know what lodge she's talking about but I'm always happy to see Zoey. She's the best sister-in-law a girl could ask for. She makes my brother smile and she's good to my mother. Plus, she's my friend. My really good author friend who always gets me advanced copies of the dirtiest books.

My brother's entire expression has changed since Zoey knocked on the door. He gestures her into the room, and she skirts around his desk, catching her shoe only once.

She settles into Brock's embrace, sitting on his lap. They fit together perfectly and I'm glad they've found each other.

I stand and take a step toward the door. Whatever she wanted to tell me about a lodge can wait until later. "I'll see you two—"

"Wait," Brock growls out. He reluctantly pulls his gaze from Zoey to me. "You're going on vacation next week."

"The Forever After Lodge is in Sweetheart, North Carolina," she explains. "My bestie, Valentine says it's beautiful. It's the perfect place to work on that project we were talking about."

I mentioned my latest project to Zoey a couple of weeks ago. But I'm still struggling with it. I want to write something that touches people's hearts, that makes them remember the characters long after the book is closed.

"Thanks, but there's still a lot to do around here," I answer, figuring I can buy myself some time. "I'll try to go on vacation next month."

Brock scowls and rakes a hand through his hair. "This can either be a request from your big brother or an order from your chief. It's time for a vacation."

"THIS CAN EITHER BE A REQUEST FROM YOUR BIG brother or an order from your chief," I repeat the words as the tiny Fiat I borrowed from the airport chugs up the curvy mountainside road to the Forever After Lodge.

I'm not even entirely sure what I'm supposed to do on vacation. At least, I'll have a tour guide while I'm here. Some woman named Gray who owns the lodge has promised to show me around thanks to Zoey.

My phone dings for the thirtieth time in the past three hours and I'm tempted to chuck it out the window. He wants me to go on vacation then insists that I text him every hour of my travel time. You'd think I was traveling naked to some inner city with high crime rates by the sheer number of texts and reminders my brother has sent.

I pull over on the side of the road and get out of the car. I need to stretch anyway. I dial my brother's phone. "You're driving me nuts," I hiss as soon as he answers. "I thought you wanted me to relax."

I have to concentrate to hear him because he's breaking up. I'm only getting every other word from him. "Then answer damn phone. Could be dead. Side of the road. You didn't. Rest area. To avoid, did you?"

This is the problem with having a brother who's worked homicide. He's seen too many stories with bad endings to be comfortable with me traveling alone.

"I'm not dead on the side of the road," I mutter as I walk the dirt road. The air here is different. It's more humid on the east coast. But there's still the slightest nip in the air. The trees around me have already started their autumn show, the leaves turning red and gold to celebrate the cooler temperatures. "I might just come back early from my vacation to kick your ass. Now *that* sounds relaxing."

"Alright, alright. Check in. Few hours," Brock says, and I feel the briefest flicker of guilt. He's trying to look out for me. He feels responsible for not being there when Dad died.

"I promise. Go annoy your wife," I insist before telling him I love him and ending the call. In the silence, I tell the trees, "He worries too much."

I walk back to the car and settle in it, checking the GPS on my phone. It loads slowly and I'm having trouble getting my data signal up here.

Fortunately, there's only an hour or so to go up the mountain road to get to the lodge but nowhere to stop along the way. At least, being a dispatcher taught me to ignore my bladder.

Even in small, safe towns like South Tahoe, there's a steady stream of callers. I eat most of my meals at my desk and face near constant adrenaline surges. It's hard to do what I do but I won't let down my dad's memory. He deserves my very best.

With that thought, I hit the button on my key fob to star the ignition. An error message displays on the dashboard: *Electronic key not detected.*

I mash the key fob two more times before it becomes very clear that the message isn't going away, and the car isn't starting. A quick search on my phone shows that the battery in the fob has most likely died. My phone battery drops low at the same time, showing off a blinking red battery icon.

"Peachy." This is almost as disappointing as the day my vibrator stopped holding a charge during the steamiest spanking scene I'd ever read.

I pocket my phone and leave the car. I'll call the rental service in the morning and tell them to send someone to get it.

Grabbing my bag and rolling suitcase with the old, loose latch, I start walking up the mountain in the direction the GPS told me to before my phone died. The entire time I'm puffing my way up the incline, I'm muttering under my breath, "Go on vacation, they said. It'll be fun, they said."

I've been walking twenty minutes when a twig snaps. I clutch my bag tighter and glance around.

Peering into the densely wooded area, I can't see anything. But the worst call I've had to take suddenly runs through my mind. The woman that called begging and pleading for someone to save her. I couldn't get help to her in time and the familiar well of tears threatens to spring up.

I swallow them down and remind myself that it's probably just a bunny or another forest animal. It's not like I'm unfamiliar with the woods. There's plenty of outdoor fun to be had in South Tahoe. Except that I'm usually inside reading.

The sounds start again, louder this time. Something is definitely in those woods. Just as I'm debating whether to seek the safety of the car, a large black bear lumbers out from the trees and onto the dirt road. It's less than twenty feet away from me and making deep grunting noises.

My mouth goes dry as the bear stands on its hind legs and begins sniffing the air. *Please don't let me smell like your next meal.*

2

GRAY

"What have we got here, Mundungus?" I ask as I slow my stroll. It's a tiny red car. Looks more like something a kid would play with than an adult would drive. Except that my sister loves her little car just like this. Fortunately, it's not her car, and the realization sends relief through me.

Today is a rare day off and I've been savoring it as I hike through the mountains of Sweetheart, North Carolina. I grew up here and I can't imagine living anywhere else. These mountains aren't just in my blood. They're in my soul.

I put my hand on the hood. "Still warm. Might be a stranded tourist nearby."

Mundungus meows softly as if agreeing. He's a stray that I adopted a couple of years ago. When he first came to me, he was all big eyes and paws with his ribs showing. Now he's at a healthy weight with a beautiful gray coat and a penchant for getting into mischief.

He sits in the pack on my back, my little adventuring buddy. Not everyone realizes cats can be great hiking companions.

I pause. I can hear something on the breeze. It's the sound of someone talking. A feminine voice, carrying on the wind, "So the thing about it is that people like me really don't taste too good. Besides, fatty foods will kill you really fast."

I have to see what the hell is going on. I take a few steps forward around the bend and my heart about stops in my chest when I see the woman talking to the black bear. It's on its hind legs, sniffing the air as she continues to babble on about the importance of eating healthy. I'm pretty sure she just started promising Jesus that she'll give up her cheese Danish obsession if he gets her through this.

"Stay quiet," I tell Mundungus and hope he listens. The noise of a small animal is the last thing this bear needs.

I step forward slowly until I'm shoulder to shoulder with the woman. Well, shoulder to chest. She's a small slip of a thing. All curves and dark ringlets pulled back in a messy ponytail. She smells fuckin' amazing too and it's a hell of a time to be realizing that.

In my deepest, most authoritative voice say, "Get gone. This ain't your home."

"Believe me, I want to go home!" She cries out as if I were talking to her.

I raise my arms and wave them slowly. "Do this."

Black bears are gentle creatures that don't like to attack people. The only time you're truly at risk of an attack is if you're dealing with a malnourished bear or you've stumbled upon a mother and her cubs. All of this information is in the pamphlets the county hands out. It's on our website too.

This bear is not only a healthy weight but he's on his hind legs and sniffing the air. At this point, he's more curious than anything. As long as it's clear to him we're not prey, there's a good chance he'll move along.

"I was going to opt for the fetal position," she whispers as she starts copying my motions.

"He'll eat your fool ass for that." You never play dead with a black bear. Grizzly, yes. But they're not located here. She's another tourist that did absolutely no research before visiting my mountain.

Her face is so white that I want to gather her up

in my arms and promise her she's safe. "Now move to the side like I am. Do not approach him or step back."

She follows my lead, careful to move in sync with me.

The bear finally finishes sniffing the air. He drops back onto all fours and saunters into the forest as if he didn't just give this woman the scare of a lifetime. She'll have a hell of a story to tell her friends when she goes back to the city.

Her shoulders slump, and she lets out a relieved breath. Her bee stung lips are just the right shade of pink and for some stupid reason, I imagine leaning down to kiss her. I wonder if they'd be just as soft and pillowy as I'm thinking.

"Thank you." She pushes back some of those ringlets and when she does, I see her hands are shaking. She's got a rolling suitcase in the middle of the road, probably left it when she saw the bear.

I move to grab the white suitcase decorated with a cherry pattern. It's cute and cheerful but the latch on it looks busted. "That car back there running?"

She shakes her head and seems to snap back into herself. "No, it just stopped. Something about the key not working. Shit, I'm glad you were here. I was so nervous. I thought I was gonna die. That bear looked like he was about to eat me and that would be a terrible vacation, not to mention my brother would never let me—"

"Let's go check out the mini mobile." I gesture for her to follow me back to the little red car.

"There's a cat on your back." She laughs like this is the craziest thing she's seen in her life. Then she just keeps laughing and laughing. That's when I realize she's probably in shock.

I shrug off the backpack carefully. It's hard to feel sad or scared when you have a kitty in your arms. At least, it always works for me. "This guy is Mundungus."

I remove him from the carrier that protects him on our adventures and the little guy immediately pushes up against her legs. He doesn't normally take to other people, but then again if she'd let me rub myself all over her body, I'd definitely take the chance.

She picks him up and strokes his fur while he revels in the attention. Lucky little bastard. "Mundungus? Like the wizard?"

At least, she's focusing on something else. "Mundungus like the furry thief who steals my sunglasses, keys, anything he can get those little paws on."

Mundungus looks up at her and meows as if he's proud of these exploits.

"I don't believe it. He's so soft and furry and sweet. I bet this little guy is the perfect angel." Her color is returning to normal and her breathing has evened out again. It eases something in my chest to see that he's calming her.

I swear Mundungus smirks at me from her arms.

"Oh, yeah. An angel with four paws. Come on, let's go see about this car." I roll her suitcase behind me and open the door for her when we arrive at the car.

As soon as she shows me the error message on the dashboard, I tell her to press the key fob to the ignition button. Just like that, the car starts. It's one of the secrets of these little vehicles. When the battery in the fob stops working, press the fob to the ignition button and the car will still sense that you have the key.

"My sister owns one of these," I explain at her delighted gasp. "You're headed to the lodge up the road, right?"

The only place on my mountain is the Forever After Lodge, a wedding venue that I own. It's a family business. Except that my drunk of a father walked out when I was a teenager. Multiple sclerosis took the once vivid, strong woman he pledged to love forever and put her in a wheelchair. So he left in the middle of the night like a coward.

She hesitates then Mundungus purrs in her arms as if reminding her that the man carrying a cat on his back can't possibly mean her any harm. "Yeah, I am. Do you know where it is? My phone battery kind of died."

Even though I already figured she was headed to the lodge, my stomach still sinks. She's most likely a bride though it's strange that she's traveling alone. Most of them show up at the lodge with their grooms or their wedding party. Heaven knows if I were lucky enough to get an angel like her, I sure as hell wouldn't let her travel alone on some mountain road where anything could happen to her.

I give her directions to the lodge, not bothering to tell her I own it. She'll figure out that one soon enough. Most of the time, I meet the brides before their big day. They come and tour the place, make sure it's what they want. But every now and then, I marry a mail order bride off to a cowboy. Must be the case here.

Evening has started to fall by the time I point her in the right direction.

Mundungus is happily resting on the passenger

seat, purring as he sleeps. He's probably dreaming of what he'll steal from me next.

She glances at the darkening sky and chews on that plump lower lip. I want to run my tongue along those little indents she's leaving behind. "Could you use a lift to the lodge? I'd rather not get lost in the dark."

I give her a nod and do my best to contort my body into the car. It's not easy and my head scrapes the roof, but I manage it.

She gives a soft giggle when I'm finally settled, and I know how ridiculous this must look. Like she's crammed a giant into a toy. A giant with a cat on his lap.

She waits until I've managed to wrap the too tiny seat belt around my big barrel chest before she starts puttering along the mountain road. "There's no chance we'll run into the bear again, right?"

It's close to hibernation season and the poor creature is probably just looking for a few last meals to stock up on. But I'm not going to tell her that. It's better if she stays distracted. "What do you do for a living?"

"I'm a dispatcher for the South Tahoe Police Department. My dad was sheriff until he passed away. Now my brother is. It's kind of a family business."

"You enjoy it?" I ask, noting the sadness in her voice. She doesn't sound all that enthusiastic and I hate the idea that she might be clocking in on a job she hates. Then again, what does it matter to me? I shouldn't be upset at the idea.

She's a bride, just like Jane. As soon as the thought floats into my brain, I remind myself to keep my distance and stay professional.

She lets out a soft sigh. "Truthfully? Not as much as I used to. But what about you?"

"I love my job," I answer. Sure, I don't believe in love. Haven't in a long time. But that doesn't mean I'm a cold-hearted bastard. I can rejoice with two people who are just hopeful enough and crazy enough to believe they'll beat the odds and have a marriage that goes the distance.

Sure, it'll probably end in divorce with at least one of them losing every material thing they hold dear and carrying life-long scars, but that's love. It leaves us a little bit damaged and a whole lot dysfunctional. Just ask any honest marriage therapist. "Where did you say you're traveling from?"

She tells me about South Tahoe, the town where

she lives and works. It sounds like Sweetheart in some ways. Both places depend on tourism dollars to keep everything running and both are quaint, little towns seemingly unaffected by the passing of time.

When she pulls the vehicle into the parking lot for the lodge, I jog around to get her door and she follows me inside. Mundungus scampers past the lobby toward my room. Well, his room. If he could talk, he'd say I'm just his guest.

The lobby is quiet tonight. Most of the staff members have the evening off since I'm not expecting a wedding party until the day after tomorrow.

Alone with her, I can't help but wonder what the lodge looks like through her eyes. I've worked hard to make it an inviting space where brides can imagine exchanging vows.

She slips her bag off her shoulder and rubs the spot where the strap was. "Do you think you could help me find Gray? She's supposed to help me get settled."

"I am Gray," I answer, frowning. Something niggles at the back of my mind. Zoey called yesterday.

Zoey Hart is a romance author that interviewed me for one of her books a few years ago. For some reason, we hit it off and became good friends. She got married a few months back, but I wasn't able to make it to the wedding.

She called me yesterday and said her sister-in-law would be coming by. She asked me to reserve her a room and show her around town. I promised to watch over her, but I'm going to have a hell of a time keeping my hands to myself with this curvy woman.

3

PIPER

"I'm Piper Parker, Zoey's friend," I tell Gray. I can't believe he's the lodge owner and my assigned tour guide for the next week. You would think he would have mentioned that on the drive up here.

He scowls and for some reason, I find that sexy. Actually, I find everything about Gray sexy. From his dark, bushy beard to his deep brown gaze. He even looks the part of a mountain man in his purple plaid shirt. He's rolled up the sleeves, revealing thick forearms with plenty of dark hair.

His big, barrel chest has me wanting to throw my arms around him and feel him squeeze me tight. He's the very definition of burly and for some reason, I can't breathe as I check him out. I try to remind myself that he's not one of the heroes from the books I read, but I can't help finding him hot.

"You didn't tell me you own the place," I say, looking around the lobby.

My mom would love the rustic feel to the place. From the wooden floorboards covered in a hand-made oval rug to the deer antlers on the wall, it's quaint and warm. There's a fireplace and over it, someone has hung dozens of pictures of happy couples. "Who are all these people?"

Gray moves to a desk in the corner. Despite his bulk, he moves with an easy grace, a man that's comfortable in his skin. "Clients who married here."

I study the picture of a woman in a white dress holding red daisies. The groom in the blue suit next to her is scowling. "Do a lot of people get married here?"

"We're a wedding lodge, so yeah. Kind of keeps the lights on." He doesn't even look up from the computer. He just continues to punch in buttons.

"Zoey didn't tell me that," I mutter. Just like she didn't tell me there are freaking black bears here. I mean, they're in the Lake Tahoe area too. But I actually expect them there and also I'm not the kind of person who does the whole hiking thing so I've never encountered one. "Who performs all of these weddings? Do you keep a priest in the basement?"

"I perform them." He's still fussing with the computer system, his blunt fingers gliding over the keys. I've never paid too much attention to a man's hands before but there's something I like about his. They're strong and gentle, capable of cradling his cat close or warding off a bear for a scared woman.

"I don't see it," I say, the words slipping out before I can stop them. This grumpy mountain man guides couples into marital bliss every day? It seems like a bit of a tall tale. I study his expression, trying to decide if he's lying to me.

But there's no amusement on his face. He picks up a keycard and passes it to me. "It's a family business. Last door on the third floor."

He walks me up to my room in silence and I wonder what to say. He seemed friendly earlier but now he's retreated behind a wall of grumpiness. "Watch for the—"

Too late, my little rolling suitcase bumps against the step and the stupid broken latch lets the contents spill out across the hall floor. Innocent things like my reading tablet and curling iron roll across the hardwood. Not so innocent things like the sexy lingerie I packed and the vibrator I tucked inside also roll across it.

I scurry to pick up as many things as I can, and Gray helps gather the items. He wraps his hand around the bright pink vibrator that surely matches the color of my cheeks right about now.

"Piper," his voice is rough as he asks the question, "Is there a boyfriend or Mr. Parker in the picture?"

"N-no," I mutter, wishing the old floorboards would part and swallow me up. I meet an incredibly hot mountain man and the first thing I do is show him my pretty panties and vibrator. This is so not how a moment like this should go.

"Good." He gently places the expensive device that's given me hours of pleasure on top of my red thong. "If you ache for something more than silicone between those pretty thighs, you come knocking on my door. I'm right across the hall."

I swallow, my mouth suddenly dry. This can't be happening. I have to be daydreaming, thinking about the hero from the book I'm writing.

But the intensity of Gray's brown gaze keeps me pinned to the spot until I finally manage to respond, "Gluh."

Which is nervous, horny single woman for: *do me now please.*

He smiles for the first time since I met him, showing off the cutest dimple I've ever seen and zips my suitcase back up. He takes my elbow and helps me to my feet until we're both standing in front of my door. "Nine o'clock tomorrow morning."

I blink up at him, wondering if that's the time he's decided when we'll do it. "What?"

Well, at least I managed a word that's actually in the dictionary. That's got to be an improvement, right?

"I'll give you a tour of the town," he answers. "That's part of the reason you're here. Research or something for a book, right?"

I nod too enthusiastically then I keep nodding and now I look like I'm a bobblehead on a dashboard. *Why can't I just be normal around hot guys?*

"Unless you'd like to scout some more black bears," he says and the only thing that gives away his teasing is the slight lift to one side of his mouth. He gestures toward the door. "Goodnight, Piper. Have sexy dreams. I know I will."

"You didn't tell me he was cute," I hiss into the phone as soon as Zoey picks up my call. There are like a million things she didn't tell me including that she sent me to a wedding lodge for my vacation. How pathetic do I look right about now?

She laughs. "I've never noticed."

"How could you not? He's all big and burly and yummy." I flop back onto the bed and wonder how she couldn't have seen him. The cord connecting my phone to the wall pulls taut and I scowl at it. "And he touched my vibrator."

"Wait, back up. How did that happen?"

I blow out a breath and tell her the story. The whole humiliating truth and the entire time Zoey is laughing so hard she's breathless.

"I'm glad you could get some amusement from the worst moment of my life." It's almost as bad as how she met Brock while she was trying to relieve herself in the snow. He saw her entire rear and everything.

"And the worst part is he's going to be showing me the sights tomorrow, so I have to pretend to be normal and not a drooling mess."

"Maybe if you're lucky, he'll show you *his* sights," she says in a tone that indicates it would be a very different kind of tour.

I snort. He had to have been teasing me earlier.

That's the only reason he'd make such an offer. He doesn't want to sleep with a twenty-two-year-old virgin that knows more about writing romance than actually living it.

He probably thinks I'm an annoying tourist he has to babysit. I figure I'll go along on his little tour for an hour or two then feign tiredness. After that, he'll feel like he's done his duty and I can enjoy the rest of my vacation in peace.

"AM I AT RISK OF SEEING MORE BLACK BEARS?" I ASK when Gray stops the truck in the parking lot for the local arboretum. When I came downstairs this morning, he said he had a full day of activities planned, but he wouldn't give me any hints. I think he likes surprising me.

"Yes." He gives me a solemn look as he turns off the truck's ignition. He already repaired my key fob for the Fiat. He had the battery changed for me when I came downstairs. "They're known to frequent the greenhouses that we'll be exploring today."

I laugh at his silliness.

"There could be a risk of an encounter if we were on the hiking trails, but we won't be using those today," he reassures me.

He leaves the truck and opens my door for me. He's done this since the moment we met, and the gesture makes me think of my dad. He always insisted I should hold out for a man that would open the doors for me, the way he did for my mom.

"Not about you being weak, pumpkin," he'd tell me in that smoker's rasp he had. "It's about treating you like the queen you are. You don't deserve nothing less."

Maybe that's why I've never dated. My dad filled my head with all these grand ideas of love, and he didn't do it by draping my mom in diamonds or giving her a fancy house. He did it by showing up in the little things, the everyday moments.

From opening her door to kissing her forehead before he left for work each morning, he cherished the woman he called his wife. He looked at my mom the same way that Brock looks at Zoey. The same way I want a man to look at me one day.

Gray guides me around the visitor's center, a cheerful blue building that has Chrysanthemums blooming in stunning hues of red, orange, and yellow. I pause to take a photo on my phone. My mom and Zoey want me to text them pictures of the sights I see. I add Brock to the chat too, so he can see that I'm on vacation.

He holds open the door to a non-descript looking greenhouse. The moment I step inside, my breath leaves my lungs in a whoosh. Behind me, I hear the door click closed as Gray stands close to me. I can feel the heat from his body but I'm too obsessed with the explosion of color in front of me. It's not just the beautiful, fragrant flowers. There are dozens of butterflies circling around them.

"This feels like a movie," I whisper, swept up by the magic.

"It's nicknamed the butterfly house. Hold out your hand like this," he says, showing me how.

I copy his motion and when a yellow butterfly lands on my fingers, I can't help giggling. "It tickles."

"That's an Eastern Tiger Swallowtail. It's our state butterfly," he explains before going on to point out the various types of butterflies in the greenhouse. Listening to his rich baritone as he talks with such affection about nature makes me smile.

"Can you take my picture here?" I ask and pass him my phone at his nod.

He positions the camera. "Say cheese."

Before I know what he's doing, he presses a soft kiss to my cheek. His beard brushes my smooth skin. It's soft, not scratchy like I expected, and I know I have to be blushing in the picture he took. *Is it possible to fall for someone this quickly?*

4

GRAY

THIS IS NOT A GOOD IDEA. I KNOW IT'S NOT. I shouldn't be trying so hard to delight Piper. I shouldn't care what she thinks or love that little blush that stained her cheeks when I took the selfie of us together. But this isn't like Jane. This is different because I put my heart all in back then. I won't make that mistake again.

"This is our next adventure?" She asks as she surveys the red awning over the tiny used bookstore. This one is my favorite and I've told myself I'm just taking her here because she's a writer. They like books and stuff, right? It has nothing to do with wanting to share one of my favorite spots with her.

"It's perfect!" She breathes before I can even

answer. She's scrambling out of the truck before I can open her door and I scowl.

I've got three sisters, so I know a woman can open her own door. But I'd still rather do it. Where I come from, it's a sign of respect and reverence for a woman.

I hurry to catch up to her, smiling at the way the breath leaves her lungs when she steps foot into the bookstore. Some people feel a sense of peace and calm when they enter a church or a garden. For me, it's a bookstore.

The familiar smell of old pages, worn carpet and coffee tickles my nose. There's a soft hum of muted voices and the squeal of a child's laughter as a little toddler delights in a book about a wiggly caterpillar. The sunlight streams through the big bay windows, illuminating the dust specks dancing in the air.

"I always feel at home in places like this," Piper tells me.

"I spent my teenage years in this store. It was my own little escape," I tell her. I don't talk much about my growing up years. They're a place I never want to go back to, a time when I was so hungry I'd search drink machines for quarters, hoping I could afford our family's next meal.

Mrs. Nancy skirts around the ancient cash

register tucked in the corner of the store and waddles toward me. She's barely five feet and nearly as round as she is tall. But she did her best to look after a hurting boy and for that, I'll always be grateful. "Look at you! Ain't seen you in forever. Lord, you're a wastin' away!"

I pat my stomach even as I feel my cheeks pinken beneath my beard. My big, burly frame has never bothered me. But I don't exactly want her calling attention to it in front of the beautiful woman I'm with. "This is Piper, Mrs. Nancy. She writes books."

"Oh, another author! What do you write?"

"Nothing published," she murmurs. "Just some little books in my spare time. Not even anything worth mentioning."

Mrs. Nancy waves a hand. "Never dismiss something that lights your soul up."

I can sense Piper's discomfort with the topic, so I tell Mrs. Nancy, "We're just going to look around for a bit. Maybe grab a couple of those pumpkin spice lattes of yours."

"Sure thing." She moves to the café area to fix us some lattes, the bracelets on her wrist rattling as she works. When she's done, I try to pay her, but she waves me off. I don't think I've ever paid for a drink or sandwich here. Mrs. Nancy simply wouldn't hear of it.

After, Piper and I wonder through the aisles of aged books with their yellowed pages and the newer books with their crinkled corners, the ones deemed no good by other booksellers because of the tiniest little flaws.

We take turns pointing out books we've read and love while we drink our weak coffee drinks. We wonder aloud what the author's inspiration was and how some books get lost to time, seemingly forgotten only to be discovered in tiny shops like this one.

We come to the display for the date with a book. Each book is wrapped in non-descript brown packaging with a note written on the outside describing the genre.

"Oh, let's do this," Piper says. She sorts through the books until she picks one that's a shifter romance and I grab a young adult fantasy. I love discovering magical new worlds. Books like these saved my life when I was a teenager so even though I might be grown, I'll always support young adult authors.

I pay for our books and guide her to the outdoor patio behind the bookstore. It's surrounded on every side by a trellis that's thick with red and gold ivy. In the center of the patio is a firepit that fills the air with the scent of woodsmoke. Surrounding the firepit are seating options including an outdoor couch and several chairs.

This place was my own personal oasis once upon a time. It still is, even though I don't get here very often.

Piper selects the couch with faded blue cushions to sit on and I'm secretly delighted that she picked a spot where I can sit right next to her. My thigh rests against her denim clad one and I have to will my cock to behave. Being so close to Piper and smelling her sweet scent is intoxicating.

Every so often, she nudges me to share a line from her book and I do the same to her. There's just something special about reading with someone else, and I love that I get to share this with her.

Hours later, we're eating sandwiches on the patio and sipping fresh coffees. "You said you spent your teenage years here."

I swallow down the last bite of tomato mozzarella panini. I debate telling her my story for a moment before deciding I want her to know. I want Piper to see me, the real me. "My mom got sick. Multiple sclerosis. My dad skipped out and that left me to take care of her and my three younger sisters. This place was my refuge in the moments when the pressure felt like it was too much to bear."

With mounting medical bills and a wedding lodge on the brink of disaster, I put my head down and got to work. Now my mama is long gone but her legacy lives on in the Forever After Lodge.

She lived to see me turn it into the premier wedding destination in the Southeast. She was the face of the whole operation but since her passing, the place has continued to flourish. She left a legacy and that's more than I can say for the man who drank himself to death.

Piper lets out a soft breath. "That sucks."

I'm grateful that she didn't tell me she was sorry. It's a catchphrase that people say when they don't know how to fill the silence after a sad story. It doesn't help. Nor do any of the useless platitudes that are offered. Everything happens for a reason. It could be worse. Time heals all wounds.

Sometimes, it's just better to acknowledge that life sucks and that you're here with the person who's suffering.

She toes off her shoes, revealing socks with little owls on them. She pulls her knees up to her chest and wraps her arms around her legs. In a soft whisper, she says, "I was always a big reader, but I got into romance books a few years ago. A call came in and this one was begging for help. She was trapped in her car, teetering on the edge of the bridge."

Tears slide down her face and I slip my arm around her shoulders. I can't give her much, but I can give her my presence and a safe place to tell her story. She sniffs and continues, "She was begging me to send help and I'm getting the information as fast as I can. But then there's this awful screeching noise and she was just gone. Went over the edge. They dragged the river, but they never found her. Sometimes at night, I can still hear her frantic cries for help."

I've always admired first responders like police officers and firefighters who rush into dangerous situations. But I'd never considered how stressful and traumatic it has to be for the dispatchers who answer the phone, the ones who can only sit and listen as horrific tragedies unfold.

"I just needed happy endings after that. Stories that could give me a reason to keep hoping, keep seeing good in the world."

"I think that's a great coping strategy." I press a kiss to the top of her head and for a long time, we sit together and don't say a word.

When the sun is finally low in the sky and there's a slight nip in the air, I tug on her hand. "Come on. I know a place not far from here."

I leave the truck parked and together we walk hand in hand down the sidewalk, dry leaves crunching under our shoes. When I open the door of the local arcade, the bell dings and I gesture toward the pinball machines. "Loser buys dinner."

For the next two hours we play, and I finally realize just how competitive my girl is. She doesn't just love winning. She loves the challenge, the thrill of the chase. The knowledge makes me smile.

She doesn't pretend she needs me to show her the shooting game and she kicks my ass soundly at air hockey. She's a woman who can hold her own and it only makes me admire her more. She's strong and determined and fierce. But she's also quiet and sensitive, a dreamer who feels everything deeply.

After our games, I buy her dinner at the drive-in. We listen to the radio and discuss our favorite movies while we eat.

I wait until I'm certain she's feeling better. I didn't realize that underneath that sunshine smile she was carrying so much pain. I feel lucky that I got a peek into her heart and I always want to guard her.

I want to be the man she reaches for when she's having a bad day.

I drive her back to the lodge after dinner, and we're in the lobby when she turns. She bumps into my stomach because I was walking so closely behind her. I suck in my stomach and grip her elbow to steady her.

"I forgot my bag," she murmurs.

"Wait here. Wouldn't want you to get eaten by a black bear," I tease before disappearing to the truck. It only takes me a second to return with her bag. I dangle it just out of reach. "Watch a movie with me tonight."

Yeah, I'd like more than a movie. But there's something about being with Piper. Her presence makes me feel like I've won the lottery and I'm eager to bask in it. Call me a selfish bastard but I want every moment of her time and all of her attention.

"Gray, is that you?" A feminine voice calls from the kitchen. It's probably Iris. She's been my best friend since we were kids. Last year, she found the love of her life and married him. But she still works at my lodge doing whatever I need. Her true passion is photography, and she takes almost all of the wedding pictures here.

Piper uses the moment of distraction to grab her

purse. She smiles up at me, regret clear in her eyes. "I should go."

Before I can answer, she floats toward the stairs.

I stand rooted to the spot, staring after her like a fool. I don't even realize I'm grinning until Iris comes into the room and I have to school my features.

"She's leaving, Gray." Though her words are a warning, her voice is soft.

"I know." My tone is casual despite the fact that her warning makes my chest feel tight. *She's just another tourist.*

She presses her lips together, her cherry red gloss brighter than usual tonight. "The same way you *knew* Jane was going to marry someone else?"

I scowl at her. I'm over Jane. But for a moment, I remember that big elaborate grand gesture. The roses. The soft piano music. The diamond I offered. Only to have her laugh in my face.

Apparently, I'm not the right kind of money. I don't have connections and a vacation home in Martha's Vineyard. I don't own a yacht or have an investment portfolio that's staggering. I'll never make the mistake of doing something like that again. I'll never be foolish enough to think that love is enough. "It doesn't matter. I'm immune to love now."

5

PIPER

I KNOW WHAT GRAY WAS REALLY ASKING ME. HE MAY have said movie but there was no mistaking the heat in his gaze. He wanted a lot more than two hours staring at a screen together. But I'm not ready. Not yet.

I try to call Zoey, but she doesn't pick up. Without a friend to talk to, I grab my laptop and open my latest book. I re-read the last scene I wrote before I remember what I'm supposed to be working on. The love scenes.

Normally, they take me forever to write. After all, it's not easy to co-ordinate the delicate dance between what a couple is experiencing physically and emotionally, to explain that soul connection to the reader.

But tonight, the scene pours from me. Word after word comes effortlessly from my fingertips. Alright, so maybe I'm imagining Gray as I write about the hero bending the heroine across the kitchen island and taking her from behind. Maybe I moan too when I imagine feeling his big, thick cock brushing against my swollen folds.

By the time I'm done writing the scene, I'm dripping. I'm aching for a big, burly mountain man with a gruff voice. I know I won't be able to sleep unless I take care of this, so I run a hot shower and grab my vibrator.

In the shower, I close my eyes and try to remember the look on his face when he touched my pink toy. Wonder. Awe. Heat. Longing.

I imagine that instead of silicone between my thighs, it's him. One of his blunt fingers teasing and caressing and pushing deep inside. He'd be standing right here, growling in my ear. Telling me he's going to get my body ready for his huge cock.

"Gotta stretch my girl wide," he'd whisper. "Your pretty cunt will take every inch. You'll like it too. Gonna feel so good when I impale you."

When I come, panting against the shower wall, it's with his name on my lips and a soft smile on my face. But then there's the hollow disappointment of realizing he's not here. He's not here for me to return the favor to or cuddle up with or talk to.

For a split second, I consider going back downstairs. Then I remember the woman calling him. She could be anybody, maybe even a girlfriend. Gray doesn't strike me as the type to take me out on the town when he has a woman. But I don't know much about the man at all.

———

THE NEXT MORNING, THE LODGE IS BUZZING WITH activity. Gray said he had a wedding party coming in today. Even though I'm sure he's just busy, it still sucks that I haven't had the chance to see him. After what we talked about yesterday, it felt like we had a connection. Maybe he just doesn't feel the way about me that I do about him.

After breakfast, I retreat to my room to work on my book some more. It's flowing well and this one feels different. It feels like magic. Maybe I'll even get up the courage to show it to Zoey this time.

I've been working on it for a few hours when there's a soft knock on my door. I stand from the armchair that overlooks the front of the lodge. I've been watching a steady stream of visitors come and go while typing away.

There's a woman with short, pink hair standing in the door. She's holding a bouquet of sunflowers and she gives me a smile. "I'm Iris. I'm the photographer here. Well, and flower delivery girl today. These are from him."

Then she's probably not his girlfriend. The thought delights me more than it should. I work to make my voice sound casual as I accept the flowers. I step back and gesture for her to come into the room. "So you work here?"

Her sneakers squeak against the wooden floor. "Yep. I've known him since we were kids."

There's no reason to be jealous of the fact that she's known him for longer or knows more about him. I set the flowers down on the chest of drawers and run my thumb over one of the soft petals. There's a tiny envelope included, and my fingers itch to open it.

She wanders to the bay windows and stares out at the growing crowd below us. They're loud, their laughter and chatter drifting up through the open window. The smell of the grill hangs heavy in the air. "The BBQ is about to start. He'd like to see you there."

"He wants to see me?" My heart beats fast as a little bit of hope blooms. Maybe I'm not the only one standing here feeling something.

She turns back to face me and sighs. She searches for the words for a long moment until she finally says, "I'm happily married to a great guy. There's never been anything between me and Gray. But he is my best friend. So, don't break his heart, OK?"

I nod and wait until she leaves to read the card. *I had a great time last night. I can't wait to see you again.*

I read the message two more times before slipping into a vintage blue dress with pink roses on it. The sweetheart neckline draws attention to my cleavage and the spaghetti straps reveal my shoulders which are my sexiest feature.

The temperatures are a little low this afternoon, so I layer a white cardigan over it. I smile at my reflection. "I think he likes you."

In school I never understood my friends who went so crazy over guys but now I get it. I understand how intoxicating it feels to like someone and know they like you back.

Downstairs, I join the party filled with smiling people. I move through the throng, trying to find Gray. I want to thank him for the sunflowers and tell him I'd like to watch a movie with him tonight. If he still wants to. Just the thought of being with him makes my palms clammy and my stomach flip but in a good way.

Something solid nudges my bare leg then Mundungus is rubbing his head along my ankle and purring. I've seen him watching the staff members with disdain today. Even when Iris tried to pet him earlier, he hissed at her. But not me. He likes me.

I lean down and pick him up, happy when he doesn't make a move to jump down. His little claw sticks in the material of my cardigan and I gently remove it. But he purrs up at me the entire time, giving me his complete trust. "You're looking so handsome tonight, Mundy. Do you mind if I call you Mundy? I think we're pretty tight, don't you?"

He meows as if responding and I can't help smiling. He's the sweetest thing I've met. My mom is a cat person, and I can't help thinking about how much she'd like him.

I glance around, trying to pick Gray out of the crowd. It shouldn't be that hard but there are so many people here and one guy around my age saunters up to me. He's wearing a Stetson and holding two beers. He offers me one.

I shake my head. "I'm looking for a friend."

"I can be your friend," he promises. He's not

leering at me so that much is good. He even has a nice smile. But he's not the big, burly guy that makes my heart beat fast.

Before I can respond Gray is stepping between us. He puts a hand on the guy's chest and says in his deep growl, "Get lost, Michael."

Michael looks at me, but I take a tiny step closer to Gray, making my choice clear.

Gray turns to me the moment the cowboy is gone. But he's still scowling. "You're mine, sunshine."

I should probably bristle at the words. It's the twenty-first century. A woman can't possibly belong to a man. But I don't bristle because the thought of being owned by the hot mountain man makes my panties damp. "What does that mean?"

He steps so close we're standing toe to toe. Or rather cute leather boot to brown work boot. "It means I want you all to myself during this vacation. I'm not sharing you with any other bastard."

"I don't want to be shared," I reassure him and my cheeks pinken as I realize all of what he said. "And I'd like the other part too."

His body language relaxes, the tension rolling from him. I think he was prepared to fight Michael and I don't know why I find that so damn sexy, but I do. There's something about knowing he'd fight to keep me that makes me feel safe and secure.

"Come on. There are people I want to introduce you to," he says.

Gray introduces me to his friends. First, there's Journey. She's the bride-to-be in tomorrow's ceremony and her groom is Cam, a firefighter. The two of them are from Courage County, a ranching town not too far from here. That's why the wedding party is so big. Almost the entire town traveled to be with them on this special day.

"How did you two meet?" I ask while Gray flips the hotdogs. He manages the grill while expertly directing a team of staff members. I don't know how he keeps everything straight and still keeps up with the conversation, but he does it. He's a born leader and it's obvious everyone looks to him.

"We met because of bull testicles," Journey explains, sending Cam a look like they have a secret they're not sharing with the world. I love it when couples do that. There's a special bond, things that only they know about each other.

"Not exactly. She spilled her beer on me, and I told her to make it up to me by going on a mechanical bull," Cam explains. His hands are on her hips, like he's anchoring her to the floor.

She's leaning back against him. She's almost purring louder than Mundy who's still in my arms. "Anyway, the prize is the ugliest pair of golden bull testicles that I've ever seen, and we won it."

"She stole them from me after we had hot sex in the women's bathroom then again in the hotel and—"

She turns and smacks him on the shoulder. It's obviously a playful swat with no malice but he quickly captures her hand and sends her a warning look. The chemistry between them is so combustible that I look away to give them a private moment.

When I glance at Gray, I find he's already staring at me. His mouth quirks up in a half grin. "What kind of cheese do you like?"

Mundy yawns in my arms, no doubt tuckered out from a day spent hissing at the staff and hiding Gray's things. Poor kitty has a rough life.

Once I tell him, he dishes me up a burger. He tries to tell me to go take a seat at one of the picnic tables.

Instead, I grab a chair and drag it near the grill. We talk while I eat, and he continues at the grill. There are too many people milling about for us to have a deep conversation, but I just like being around him. Judging from the way he keeps looking at me, I think he likes it too.

It's late when the guests have finally started to retire. Gray's spent the day on his feet, making food for the whole town of Courage County. He's also handled so many staff questions and prevented more than one catastrophe. He looks nearly dead on his feet and now he's cleaning up the grounds, carefully picking up trash.

When we're done, he walks me up to my room. The lodge is different tonight. With more people in it, I can hear the quiet hum of conversations, footsteps on the hardwood floors and children squealing in laughter. Tonight, the lodge is alive and cozy.

We're alone and in front of my door so if this goes terribly wrong, I can retreat in there and pretend I didn't make this offer. I figure that makes it as good a time as any to shoot my shot. "Hey, Gray?"

"Yeah, sunshine?"

The way he says the nickname fills me with warmth. He makes me feel so safe and protected. That's how I find the courage to blurt out, "Maybe we could watch a movie tonight?"

6

PIPER

"Are you sure?" His voice is deep, but I don't let myself glance at his face.

Goosebumps skitter along my skin and it has nothing to do with the cool night air and everything to do with this sexy man. "I want you."

He puts a finger under my chin, tipping up my face. His gaze searches mine for a long moment. But whatever he sees there must reassure him because he gives me a soft smile. "I want you too."

My mouth goes dry at the way he's staring at me. OK, wow, this is really happening. Suddenly, I think of a million things I should have done. I mean my legs are shaved. But I definitely have some landscaping to handle and I bet I smell sweaty from being outside all afternoon.

He slides his hands around my hips, pulling me close. I love the way I can feel him against me, his big chest and his even bigger...oh. *Oh.*

Backup. A girl definitely needs backup.

"I need a girly minute," I say softly. I'm probably ruining the moment. I'd planned to be this cool, calm seductress. Instead, I'm still me, the geeky girl that doesn't know what to do with a hot guy.

"Girly minute?" He repeats, a frown creasing his face.

"Yeah, just five minutes," I murmur before I step backwards. I bump into my door and reach for the handle fumbling with it.

He reaches around me and opens it. "Piper—"

"Just five minutes." I hold up my hand to indicate the five minutes before disappearing into the room. As soon as I shut the door, I let out a breath. It's official. I'm a disaster when it comes to this stuff.

With shaky hands, I reach for my phone. I dial Zoey but she's not there. I try Cleary, my friend from the police station, and still no dice. *What does a girl have to do to reach her squad?*

"It's OK," I tell myself. "We'll start with the shower anyway."

But twenty minutes later, the shower water is running and I'm just standing in the bathroom fully clothed. I'm staring off into space and wondering if I wait long enough if Gray will forget about what I said.

A knock on the door startles me but before I can say anything, Gray is coming in. He sees me standing here and I offer a pathetic shrug. I have to swallow around a lump in my throat. *He's figured it out.*

When I risk a glance at his face, his expression is soft. "Why are you hiding from me, sweet girl?"

The quiet stretches between us, the only sound is the rush of the shower water. The white noise fades and finally I admit in a whisper, "I've never…I mean, I'm on birth control. But I don't know how to do *this*."

I'm twenty-two years old, and I've never slept with a man. Why didn't I just get it over with and lose my virginity in high school? Then maybe I wouldn't be standing here in front of the hottest guy I know and thinking that I'm going to mess this up.

He crosses from the doorway to stand in front of me. He wraps his arms around me, pulling my body close. For a long moment, he just holds me before saying, "That's OK. We'll learn together."

I lean back to search his face. "Learn together? Does that mean…?"

"That I'm a thirty-year-old virgin about to have

sex for the first time? Yeah, it does." Amusement crosses his features. Our society applauds men who have multiple sexual partners, viewing it as a sign of their prowess. Yet he's owning this so casually, like it's not a big deal at all.

I relax at his confession. He's new at this, just like me. Somehow, that knowledge eases the knot in my stomach.

He rubs my back in a circle, his fingers working magic on my muscles. "How about we just have fun together?"

I put my head against his chest. He's solid and strong, dependable and steady. "I was about to shower. I wanted to smell good for this."

"Then we'll shower," he answers. He lets me go, stepping back so he can help me shrug out of my cardigan. I toss it onto the bathroom vanity, not caring where it lands.

When he realizes the zipper is in the back, he turns me. His hands are so large, but every touch is gentle. His fingers caress the bare skin of my back as he drags it down, inch by agonizing inch.

I want to see the look in his eyes when he sees me naked for the first time. Facing him, I peel the dress off. It gets stuck on my hips once and I have to shimmy to get it down. It pools in the floor at my feet.

With my heart in my throat, I glance up at Gray. But he's staring down at me with a look of complete fascination. More than that, he's gripping himself through his jeans. I wonder if he even realizes he's doing it.

"So beautiful," he murmurs. He reaches out a hand to trace my collarbone before dipping it lower and lower. He cups my breast through my thin, lacy bra and runs his thumb along it. My nipple hardens even more.

I let out a strangled gasp. "Your turn."

He unbuttons his shirt quickly and tosses it on the floor before reaching for the button of his jeans. But something's bothering me, and it takes me a second to figure out what it is. He's avoiding my gaze, and I realize maybe he feels just as exposed as I do.

I trail my fingertips down the center of his wide chest, pausing to rub his sternum. "You're so strong. It made me feel safe when you stood between me and Michael."

He snaps his eyes to mine and I see the relief in them. His cheeks pinken beneath his beard. It finally occurs to me that my mountain man isn't grumpy.

He's just shy. "I'll always stand between you and the rest of the world."

My heart soars at the words and I reach for his button, biting down on my lip. I manage to fumble his pants open. I gasp when his cock springs free. He's definitely bigger than my toy.

I start to reach for him, but he captures my hand. "Not yet."

Gray tugs me toward the shower and helps me into it. As soon as the door swings closed and we're cocooned in the warmth of the shower, my body relaxes even more. A thrill runs through me. I'm here and I'm naked. With this sexy guy who likes me back.

He unclasps my bra and pulls down my panties, both of them landing in the shower floor. Then he guides me under the shower spray and washes my hair. I love the way he's touching my scalp and massaging in the shampoo. He takes his time, like we have all of it we need. He's not rushing this and he's looking at me like he enjoys taking care of me. Is it possible he's starting to feel something deeper, the same way I am?

He grabs my purple loofah and washes my back then my front. He pays special attention to my breasts, kneading them and running his hands along them.

"So pretty," he murmurs as he circles my nipples with his thumbs.

Moisture has started to get between my thighs and my body is hot and achy. I feel restless, almost as if my skin is too tight.

Gray sets the loofah aside and drops to his knees in the tub. He glances up at me once, searching my face. I don't know what he's looking for, but I give him a little nod. Knowing that we're exploring together makes this special in my eyes.

He kisses my stomach, and I expect him to go for my pussy. But he doesn't. Instead, he works his way down my legs, ignoring that spot where I'm aching. He kisses me all the way down to my ankle before starting his way back up. By the time he's reached my knee, I've spread my legs. I'm ready for whatever he wants to give me.

"Is my sweet girl horny?" He murmurs against my skin.

That soft feeling of his beard is heavenly. I need to feel him against my pussy. Need him to give me what he's teasing me over. I whimper in response.

"I've got you," he whispers. He presses kisses

higher and higher until he stops and inhales deeply. "Damn, you smell good."

It's the last thing he says before he licks my slit, and I nearly collapse. Alright, I've read about this stuff. Hell, I've written about it. But nothing compares to the feeling of having Gray on his knees in front of me with his tongue teasing my soft folds.

He slowly works me into a frenzy until I'm pulling on his hair and rubbing myself into his face. He makes obscene growls as he eats me out, and I'm pretty sure he's making dirty promises against my swollen flesh, but I'm too far gone to listen to what he's saying.

The orgasm rolls me through quickly and fiercely, like a summer thunderstorm that comes on suddenly. Everything else fades except until I can only focus on this moment right here with Gray.

My knees buckle but he's already on his feet, wrapping an arm around my waist. His face and beard glisten with my essence. He pushes a strand of hair back from my forehead and stares down at me for a long moment. "You alright there?"

I manage a nod, my whole body is boneless, and I don't even try to support myself. I just let Gray hold me close, reveling in the way it feels to be naked with him.

After a moment, he leaves the shower long enough to grab the fluffy towel on the hook. He wraps it around me and picks me up in his arms. I try to tell him to put me down, but he just laughs. "Never letting you go."

"You're going to carry me around for the rest of time?" I tease.

His brown eyes are lighter than they were earlier tonight. He looks happy and relaxed, the same way I feel. "Yeah, I'll put you in my pocket. Carry your cute, tiny ass around everywhere."

I wiggle out of his arms and onto the bed. I shrug out of the towel and lie back on the bed, spreading my legs. "Well, before you put me in your pocket, maybe there are some other things we should do first."

7

GRAY

THIS IS HEAVEN. MY GIRL ON HER BACK WITH HER LEGS spread, her pussy dripping. She's soaked for me. Waiting for me.

I crawl over her body, careful when I position myself to keep my weight off of her. She might be curvy but she's still so much smaller than me. She's delicate and I'd die before I hurt her. I sure as hell wouldn't let anyone else touch her. I about lost my mind today when I saw Michael looking at her.

"You're scowling again." She reaches up to touch my face. The simple motion instantly soothes me. Any time she touches me, it calms me.

"I hate Michael," I grind out.

"Please tell me he's not the one you're thinking about right now." There's a teasing lilt to her voice.

"I'm thinking about the way he looked at you. Like he could take what's mine." The idea has me wanting to go to fuckin' war. She belongs to me. She belongs with me. I want her by my side.

She rubs her fingertips along my back. "He never stood a chance. He never will."

The words are just what I need to hear. I let out a soft sigh and kiss her slowly, tracing her tongue with mine. I want her body more than I've ever wanted anything in my life. But I'm not so far gone or so selfish that I won't make it good for her.

I kiss her until she's squirming beneath me and begging for my cock. Fuck, there's no better sound than Piper begging me to fill that little pink hole of hers.

Carefully, I align our bodies. I mean to go slow, to take this easy. But the moment I feel her wet heat sucking me in, my control snaps. I slam into her with the force of a hurricane.

"How does that feel?" It feels fuckin' perfect to me. She's squeezing me so tightly, her walls clamping down on my thick cock as she takes me raw.

"So good," she moans. "More."

Her words are all I need. I lose myself in a haze of pleasure, thrusting deep into her channel only to pull out and do it again and again. I play with her clit, wanting her to come again too. I won't last long but I can make this good for her at least.

When she comes, I follow her over the edge. My seed shoots deep into her pussy, filling her up and marking her as mine. Just like that, it feels like something has shifted in my life. I can't describe it and I don't bother to examine it too closely. That's what the morning is for. Right now, I just want to hold this beautiful woman.

I WAKE TO THE SOFT SNORES OF PIPER AND CAN'T HELP smiling. After we drifted to sleep last night, she woke me twice in the night to take her. We spent more time fucking than we did sleeping, and I don't regret any of it.

I'd love to wake her with kisses and spend a long morning between her thighs. But Journey's wedding is today, and I'm the officiant. If it were anybody else, I might try to get a staff member to officiate the wedding.

This is Journey though. She's like a little sister to me. She requested me, so I'll do it without question.

Maybe later, after the festivities are over, I can sneak back here with Piper.

I nuzzle her ear. "I have to go, sweet girl."

She murmurs sleepily, something about going with me.

"No, you sleep. But I'll be missing you," I reassure her. I want her to know that even if I can't be with her right now, I'm still thinking of her. She's been the only thing on my mind since the moment she's arrived. I don't want her doubting that for a minute.

She burrows back into her pillow without another word and she's softly snoring again a few seconds later.

I chuckle as I roll from the bed. My body might be exhausted, but I've never had more energy. The day has never felt brighter, and life has never seemed quite as beautiful as it does today.

Even after I've handled several minor emergencies for the wedding, I'm still feeling upbeat as I stand in front of the bride and groom.

Journey and Cam promise their love for each other. They chose traditional vows, ones I've heard a thousand times before. But as I look out over the guests in attendance, I scan the crowd. When my gaze lands on Piper, I can't help smiling.

I wonder what it'd be like to have her here

every night. It'd be fucking perfect to have her in my bed. To crawl into it late at night and know her tight, curvy body is waiting for me. To take her to my favorite bookstore during the mornings and lose to her at air hockey and come back to the lodge to share a meal together. I can see it all at once.

My mouth goes dry and my hands get clammy. I might want that but there's no way she wants a backwoods mountain man like me. I'm just the vacation fling, the guy she'll be with before she goes on to find someone else.

I pronounce Cam and Journey husband and wife as cold dread slithers through me. I'm an idiot. I've made the same fuckin' mistake twice in my life.

Piper approaches me at the reception. We need to have a talk and I know this. But right now isn't the time or the place.

"Want to dance?" She gives me a carefree grin. I'm the funny story she tells her friends before she marries the man that will get to hold her every night.

Swallowing down the bile, I shake my head and manage to mutter something about how much work I still have to do.

Her expression falls and for a moment, I want to believe this is real. I want to believe that she cared about me. But I'm being ridiculous. "Oh, maybe later then."

Piper

GRAY HASN'T TALKED TO ME ALL DAY. I KNOW HE WAS busy working when I asked him to dance. I know he has a lot going on when there's an event. But yesterday, he made time for me. He kept chatting with me even as he managed all the chaos of the lodge.

Still as the hours pass, I eventually retreat to my room. I wait for him here but something tells me he's not coming back to my bed.

Mundy meows at my door and I open it to let him in. He lays something at my feet, and I lean down to pick up the shiny square plastic. That's when I realize what this is. It's the keycard for Gray's room. "You are a little thief."

He meows as if he's done nothing wrong.

Taking the card, I slip into the room across the hall. Since Gray isn't going to come to me, I'll just wait for him.

It's nearly midnight and I've been asleep for over an hour when I hear the rattle of a doorknob. I spring away and rub the sleep from my eyes. I have to figure out what went wrong. Why was Gray so nice to me earlier and now he can't stand to look at me?

He pauses when he sees me on the bed, curled up next to Mundy. "You didn't have to wait up for me."

I rub the sleep from my eyes and blink at him. Where's the man from last night, the one who looked at me like I was his whole world? I don't think he's still in there because the person I'm looking at right now feels like a stranger. "I missed you."

He looks away from me, his gaze roaming the room. "Yeah, about that. Last night was…"

I fold my arms over my chest and wait. I'm not rescuing him from this. He can say whatever he wants but he can't lie to me. I know what I saw on his face last night.

"It was a one time thing. Nothing more," he finally finishes.

My heart splinters into a million pieces. Can he hear the sound of my heart cracking open? I shake my head. "Bullshit. I saw the way you looked at me last night. You felt it too. You're just a coward."

"A guy will say and do anything to get into your pants." He laughs and it's a cruel sound. "Did you really believe it was my first time? Were you naïve enough to believe what I said?"

I swallow around the lump in my throat. I will not cry in front of him. I will not let him see me break down. Our night together was so special. He was so gentle with me and it was all an act. "You were lying about that?"

He finally looks at me. His face is a mask of indifference. "You didn't think you it meant something, did you? Hell, you write fairytales for a living. You should know better than that."

"Yeah, I guess I do know better than that now. Thanks for the lesson." With that, I stalk across the room. My back is ramrod straight and I don't even let myself look at him as I step around his bulky frame to leave the room.

I know better than to navigate that mountain road at night, so I go to my room and I pack my things. Then I sit in front of the window and wait for the sun to rise. I won't let myself cry. I won't give him the satisfaction of hearing my tears through the wall.

As the first ribbons of light begin to break through the darkness, I grab my suitcase. My vacation is over. It's time to go home.

8

PIPER

"CHECKING OUT SO SOON?" IRIS FROWNS AT ME. "I thought your reservation was for longer."

I give her a serene smile and reach for the same calm I do every time a call from a panicked resident comes in. "Turns out I'm needed back home. Police department can't function without me."

She hasn't stopped frowning, but she seems to accept my answer. "I hope everything is all right. We'd love to see you again here."

My cheeks ache from smiling but I make chit chat with her until the transaction is processed. But it's not until I'm sitting in the airport that I can breathe. I will myself to hold it together for a few more hours.

The plane ride is the longest one of my life and when I finally touch down back in California I know I'm home. But I don't feel like I'm home. Because home feels like Gray's arms around me. Except he doesn't want me.

The moment I'm at my house, I take a shower and throw my clothes in the wash. I need the smell of this lodge off of me. When I'm done, I send out a text to Zoey and Cleary. I don't tell them what happened, just that I'm home already.

Within fifteen minutes, they're on my front porch. They've brought ice cream and wine. I must look pretty rough because they wrap their arms around me in a group hug and that's the moment that the dam finally breaks.

We settle on the couch together and I pour out the whole story. From the start with the black bear all the way to Gray's sudden change in behavior. "I don't understand him. I couldn't have misread it that badly, could I have?"

Before they can answer, there's a knock on my front door then Brock is barreling in the house. He's wearing his big brother scowl and I realize that Zoey must have texted him. He takes in my tear-stained face. "Fuck that loser. He doesn't deserve you. I'm going to call him. What's his number, Zoey?"

"Don't do that," I protest. My heart is bruised but I'm not going to get my brother to bully Gray into saying he likes me. That would be humiliating. More humiliating than the current situation.

"You're right." Brock nods decisively. He yanks his phone from his pocket and calls his assistant at the police station. "Marge, I want the first plane ticket out to Asheville and rent me a car at the airport. I'm going to kick ass for my sis—"

I look to Zoey and she stands from the couch. She snatches the phone from Brock. He's so much bigger than her. He doesn't have to surrender it to her, but he's wrapped around her little finger. She only has to give the word and he does whatever she commands.

"Marge," she says into the phone, "Cancel that. Yeah, everything is fine. I'll call you back later."

Brock turns his focus back to me. "What did he do to you?"

I shake my head sadly. "He didn't do anything. He just...doesn't feel the same way about me."

Gray

"You're moping," Iris says as she flops down in the chair across from my desk. This is the lodge office where I handle all the official business. Lately though, I don't handle much. I just stare off into the distance.

I continue sorting through the mail, not bothering to look up. It's been two days since Piper left. I think it's been two days. It's felt more like ten years. Every breath hurts and all I want is her back in my arms.

"Come into the kitchen," she says.

"Not hungry." I'm existing now, a shell of myself. I keep saying that I'll feel better tomorrow but deep in my gut, I already know the truth. I'll never feel the same again. Piper was it for me.

"I said come into the kitchen." Her tone tells me she's not leaving me alone until I do what she says.

I grumble under my breath and toss the mail onto my desk. I can finish that later. If I remember to. I'm not sleeping at night and my memory is becoming crap.

I follow Iris into the kitchen the staff uses to prepare the food. There's a wooden table in the corner where the staff will stop and eat as time allows. But instead of staff members sitting around the table, my three sisters are here. As soon as I see them, I turn around. But she snags me by the shirt. "Sit. Down."

I scowl and move to the kitchen table, taking the empty spot next to Ava. She's the youngest and I've always been close to her. "This feels like an intervention."

"Good!" Iris claps her hands together. "Then you know where this is going."

I fight a wave of dread. My sisters are happily married. They believe in love and fairytales and all of that stuff. I'm happy for them. I want them to have the best in life and that means I worked damn hard over the years to keep them from feeling the brunt of my father's absence. I was the one who taught Ava how to throw a softball and threatened Sophia's prom date into being a gentleman. I taught Luna how to drive a stick shift and apply to college.

Sophia frowns at me. "Gray, what happened?"

"There was a girl," Iris says before I can brush off my sisters' concern and get back to work. "Gray liked her, and she liked him back."

Ava gasps. "What happened?"

"He messed it up!" Iris really should have been a lawyer. "He sent her away."

"I didn't send her away. She left," I defend, looking to Luna. She's the oldest and the one who will understand. She was abandoned at the altar before she found her perfect match. I spent months picking up the pieces and helping her before she discovered the strength to start putting herself out there again. If her groom-to-be hadn't skipped town, he'd have been in traction by the time I was done with him. No one makes my sisters cry.

"After you messed up!" Iris smacks her hand down on the table, always the one for the dramatics.

"All I did was cut my losses. We were never going to work."

Ava runs a hand through her pixie cut hair. I taught her to throw a punch when she was in third grade because one of the boys wouldn't leave her alone. I was probably more like a father to her than I was to Luna or Sophia. "Is this about Jane?"

"Who's Jane?" Luna demands.

Fuck me, I got drunk with Ava one night and the whole sordid story with Jane came out. I never meant to tell anyone about it. "No one. She was just a bride that came to the lodge years ago."

"He fell in love with her. Like head-over-heels, name-a-star-after-her type of love," Ava explains. "She was planning her wedding but the entire time she was stringing along Gray and telling him she was having doubts about her upcoming marriage. So your brother here went all out and gave her the proposal of a lifetime and she laughed in his face, the bitch."

"And you're worried that will happen again." Sophia nods, the bun on her head bobbing as she does. She runs a craft and yarn shop in downtown Sweetheart.

"Did you talk with her about any of this?" Luna presses.

I push away from the table and get to my feet. Talking about this isn't doing me a damn bit of good. "I have a lodge to run."

For the next few hours, I hide away in my office. I keep the door locked and wait until the sounds of the lodge have quieted before I finally breathe. That's when there's a knock on my door. "It's me. Luna."

I debate not answering, but I won't hurt my sister's feelings for the world. So I unlock the door. She passes me a mug of my favorite cinnamon coffee. "Can I come in?"

I grunt my acceptance and open the door. She did bring me caffeine after all.

Luna takes a seat on the couch across from my

desk. She wraps herself in the blanket on the back, bringing back years of memories. She used to hang out in here when she was having an anxiety attack. She'd play music on her phone while I worked at the desk. "It always looks the same in here."

I lean back in my chair, feeling the familiar throbbing in my temples. Since I'm not sleeping, I keep near constant headaches. Even the strongest coffee won't chase them away.

"You never told me about Jane," she says softly.

I shrug. I've thought a lot about this over the past few hours, about why I didn't tell them. "I was embarrassed. I put my whole heart in, and she didn't want a backwoods mountain man."

"It's hard to put yourself out there again," she says. After Harrison left her at the altar, she fell in love with Kasey but wouldn't admit it. Not that it mattered. He chased her for over a year. He knew when he laid eyes on her that he'd love her forever. Maybe that's why her scars never scared him.

I set my empty coffee mug on the desk and study her. "How did you do it?"

"There was this moment when I realized I couldn't imagine my life without him and that's when I knew I had to try again."

I think of how bleak my life seems now. I can't

muster up the energy to look forward to anything. There's only the yawning chasm of the coming years and the loneliness that will follow me until the day I'm buried. "I want Piper, but she doesn't want me." Admitting that out loud makes me feel raw and exposed, like she's seeing everything in my heart.

"Did she say that?" Luna prompts.

"She didn't have to. She'd say it at some point." The loss would have crushed me. I'd never recover from Piper.

Luna's tone is soft as she asks the probing questions. "So, did you actually give her the chance to reject you? Or did you just make the decision for her?"

"I love her." My voice cracks on the words. With Jane, I wasn't scared. I was so convinced she felt the same way that it never occurred to me that she'd still marry the senator's son with the million-dollar trust fund.

"Then you need to give her a chance to love you back," Luna says. "Love requires bravery and vulnerability and risk. And when it all goes wrong, it hurts like hell. But that moment when you find the one person meant for you—the one who loves you back —that makes it all worthwhile."

I'm quiet for a long time as her words sink in. "You're saying I fucked up."

"Yeah, but it's probably not beyond repair."

I nod and take a deep breath. "Then I'll need a favor. A big one."

9
PIPER

I finished the book. It's not my first completed book but it's the one I'm proud of. I want to share it with other people, and I'm ready to take that step. I have some money in savings. Dad wasn't rich but he left me a small inheritance. I've kept it in savings and let it grow for a while because I didn't know what to do with it. I do now.

"What is this?" Brock looks up from the paper he's holding in his hands. It's my resignation letter. "Is this about the vacation? Look, I'm man enough to admit that it's my fault that happened."

It's been over a week since I went away to the Forever After Lodge. Every day, I'm greeted with a new delivery of sunflowers at work and another one at home. Each time, I donate them and throw the unread note in the garbage. I don't want to read Gray's lame apology or other excuses. He made it clear he was only in it for sex. Well, he got what he wanted.

"No, the vacation was exactly what I needed. I want to honor Dad's memory, but I'm not happy here. Not anymore."

He lets the paper flutter onto his neat desk. The two of us finally finished digitizing the files last week. "Is that why you've stayed all this time, trying to be strong for Dad?"

"I know it sounds silly when I say it out loud, but it felt like I was keeping him alive by staying." The more I thought about it, the more I realized he wouldn't want me to stay for that reason. My dad always encouraged me to follow my dreams. He never forced the station life on me. I chose it and up until he passed away, I was always content with that choice. Now though, it reminds me of how much I miss him.

Brock nods. "If this is what you want, then I'm happy for you. But what are you going to do with your time?"

I give him a small smile. "I'll write books. Live off

what Dad left. It's not much but I won't have to eat cheap noodles either."

"He'd be proud of you for finding a new dream." He gestures toward the letter. "Guess I gotta put the word out that I'm looking for a new dispatcher."

"I'll work until you've finished training the new hire." I push to my feet. It'll be weird not to see my big brother and police friends every day. But it's time to do this. Time to start pursuing new dreams. I only wish those dreams included a certain lodge owner.

Brock moves around his desk too, and in an uncharacteristic show of emotion, he hugs me close. "Be happy, Pip."

I smile at his old nickname. Things may not have turned out the way I wanted them to in my love life, but I have an amazing support system. I'm leaving my job to pursue a dream I've always wanted to. I have a lot going for me.

Moving back to my desk, I take a seat beside Cleary. "Did you do it?"

I let out a slow breath and nod.

She gives me a thumbs up but before she can say more, the bell above the door rings signaling that someone has stepped into the police department.

Our cubicles are by the front entrance, so I only have to look up to see who's entering. Given the location of the dispatch desks in the office, it's common to have to direct visitors to the various areas.

But this time when I look up, my heart skips a beat. Standing in front of me is Gray holding a bouquet of sunflowers. I blink but he doesn't disappear. Is this real? Is he here? Or am I having another one of those dreams where he shows up?

He scans the office and when his gaze finally lands on mine, time stops. How is it that we've been apart for over a week and he still looks so damn good? Then again, I guess that's what happens when your heart isn't the one that's broken.

"Another flower delivery?" Cleary asks in her crisp, professional tone. She knows the flowers are from Gray. She doesn't know that he's flown across the country to deliver this particular bouquet. But like all the others, it'll be donated to the local hospital.

I duck my head and pretend I'm busy entering data into my computer.

"I'm here for Piper," he says in that deep, rumbling voice he has. I remember the way he wrapped his arms around me in the shower. The dirty things he murmured as he pressed kisses along my heated flesh.

"You can put them wherever you want, Gray." I keep my gaze on the screen, relieved when my tone comes out cool and unaffected. I haven't acknowledged any of the deliveries before this and I'm not about to start now.

Cleary's eyes go wide and before I can say anything else, her fingers twitch. It's the slightest move but I think she just hit the panic button. It'll send the station into instant lockdown. It was a system designed to keep a criminal from escaping the building.

A half second later, my guess is confirmed when three police officers tackle Gray and take him down to the ground. The flowers are crushed in the ensuing chaos, smushed between his big chest and the faded linoleum.

I stand so quickly that my chair rolls backwards. "Stop! Stop! The button was hit by mistake. He's not a criminal!"

By this point, Brock is out of his office and his officers look to him for guidance, awaiting a word from their chief. But my brother is focused on me. "What's going on here?"

"That is Gray from the lodge," Cleary answers

with a little too much delight. She's always had a thing about justice. It wouldn't surprise me if in her spare time, she were one of those superheroines that goes about the town dishing out justice. I could totally see her in a cape and mask, stealing from the rich to provide for the poor.

"Let him up." Brock's voice is made of steel.

The officers don't hesitate to obey their leader. They take off the cuffs and one of them lifts their knee from Gray's back. In their defense, they thought he was a threat and responded according to their training.

They help him onto his feet and Gray straightens his plaid shirt. He scowls. "Heck of a response team you got, Sheriff."

"You have ten seconds to get out of here before I find a real good reason to arrest you," he answers.

Gray looks to me, his brown gaze searching mine. I remember the way he looked so happy when we settled on the patio at the bookstore, how we sat together and read for hours. If there were ever a perfect date, that was it. "I'm here for her."

I continue standing but don't bother to dismiss the officers. Whatever he wants to say to me can be said in front of these strong men that won't hesitate to tackle him again if he makes me cry. "What do you want?"

"I'm an asshole." He raises his voice, making sure everyone in the office can hear him. No one is even pretending to work anymore. They're all staring openly at us. Especially Brock who has his hands on his hips. I imagine it's taking all of his self-restraint not to throttle this mountain man.

"An obvious conclusion," I mutter. Several people snicker but my goal isn't to humiliate Gray.

Despite our audience, he never looks away from my face. It's like we're the only two people in the room to him. "I've been hurt. When I realized I was falling in love with you, I was scared of that happening again. So I pushed you away, and fuck, I've regretted it every moment since. I know I don't deserve a second chance with you but I'm asking for one anyway."

I want to reach for this second chance with him so badly. But my heart hurts too much. "You acted like I didn't matter. I can't do that again."

"Never again," he promises as he steps around the desk and into my space. "Never again will I guard my own heart instead of yours. From this moment forward, your heart will always come before mine. You're it for me, Piper Parker. I love you, and whether we're together or not, you'll be mine for the rest of my life."

"Gray..." Tears spill down my cheeks despite my resolution not to cry.

He reaches out to catch one of the tears on his finger. "I'm signing away the lodge to my sisters, and moving here. They can run it without me. But I can't live without my sunshine."

"I love you too." I hiccup softly.

A soft smile crosses his face. "I'll spend the rest of my life—"

I press a finger to his lips. "I don't want you to make anything up to me. We're together now and that's in the past."

He presses a soft kiss to my fingertip. "Yeah, we're together now."

Then despite our watching audience which includes my brother, Gray brushes his lips against mine. It's soft and gentle at first. But then I grip the front of his plaid button down and that's all it takes. His tongue is sweeping into my mouth and I'm pushing against him, trying desperately to get closer.

I don't even realize anyone has cleared their throat until he's pulling away from me.

Brock is scowling at the two of us. Actually, I think he's scowling at Gray. "You ever pull a stunt like this and you'll drink all your meals for the rest of your life while someone changes your diapers. You got that?"

"She's my whole world," Gray answers.

I can't help the grin that stretches across my face when he says that. Because this mountain man in front of me? He's my whole world too.

EPILOGUE

GRAY

I PUT ANOTHER BOX IN MY TRUCK. IN JUST A FEW minutes, I'm about to drive cross-country with my wife. It's been six months since I begged her forgiveness in the middle of the police station and one week since we got married.

It's hard to manage the lodge remotely. I thought handing it off to my sisters would be a smooth transition. There have been a lot of bumps along the way and the truth is I miss my hometown.

Still when Piper suggested that we move there, I hesitated. I don't ever want her to be unhappy for any reason. But the more we talked about it, the more I realized she was excited by the idea.

Piper's writing career is taking off. She publishes a lot of romance books. Her best-selling ones all happen to be about studly mountain men who are grumpy and claim their curvy woman. In each dedication, she thanks me for being her real-life inspiration.

Her brother Brock had just started to warm to me then I proposed to Piper and the warmth faded. He finally accepted the idea that we were getting married and warmed to me again. Now he knows that Piper is moving halfway across the country to help me run the Forever After Lodge. At this rate, I'm pretty sure he's going to spend the rest of his life hating me. Not that I can blame him. Piper is one of a kind.

"Are you sure about this?" I ask after I've secured another box. We've only been living together a few months and we've still managed to amass a staggering amount of household items.

"Do you want me to stay behind?" She pouts.

I grab her around the waist and pick her up in my arms. I press a kiss to her temple and whisper in her ear, "Do you want me to prove how much I want you to go with me?"

She shivers. "Yes, please."

Inside her house, there's only one piece of furniture still assembled. Our bed. I was supposed to take it down earlier this morning but given my habit of making sure my wife orgasms at least twice a day, I figured I could put that off for a little while.

I set her down, gently. Reverently. She's the most important person in my world. Hell, she is my world.

She reaches for her clothes and quickly removes them. Six months together and she knows I adore her body. I worship every inch of her skin and regularly remind her of how sexy she is.

As soon as we're both naked, I press soft kisses everywhere I can get my lips until she's writhing and begging me for it. Doesn't matter if I'm licking that pretty pussy or ramming my thick cock into it, my favorite place will always be between her thick thighs.

"Need you," she gasps.

"Tell me what you want," I murmur, nipping at her shoulder. She likes having her shoulders played with, so I always give them extra attention any time we're together.

"Your cock," her words are a moan. "Can't wait."

I line up our bodies, teasing her with just the tip for a long moment. But then she hooks her leg around my hips. "Give it to me."

I thrust into her quickly, filling her up in one smooth motion. She cries out as I begin rocking in and out of her greedy channel. "So good to me, sunshine. You're always so good to me."

"More," she murmurs. Her gaze is glassy and unfocused, telling me she's close to the edge already.

I slip a hand between our bodies and stroke her clit with the pad of my thumb. That's all it takes and she's bucking against me, milking my cock and sending me into my own release. As my come shoots deep into her womb, she lets out a little sigh.

I collapse beside her in the bed, pulling her into my arms. "I love you."

"Love you, too." She snuggles deeper into my embrace. Our walls are as bare as we are. I've never been a decorations guy. Never cared much what my spaces looked like, but I miss the collage of wedding photos she had by our bed. I love seeing those as I drift off to sleep at night and again every morning. To me, those photos are proof that my dreams can come true. Every single one of them.

I've already made it clear to Piper that our wedding photos are the first thing I want up in our new place. I used to live in the lodge and that worked great when I was single.

Since marrying the love of my life, I want a place that's just ours. A place where we can grow a family one day. So I had a custom cabin built about a mile down the road from the lodge. I made sure that Piper was consulted on every step along the way. It's her forever home and I want her to be happy there.

"What are you thinking about?" She asks as she runs her fingertips along my arm.

"Our new home," I answer. Her home is beautiful, but the tiny place isn't ideal for the big family I want and there's no writing nook for her. She doesn't know it yet, but I talked with the builders and had them add on a sunroom where she can write. She has a vision board of what she wants her dream office to look like and I simply copied everything on it.

"There are a lot of bedrooms in it," she murmurs. "We'll have to fill them one day, don't you think?"

My heart beats fast and with her head on my chest, I wonder if she can hear it. She might even notice the tremble in my voice when I say, "The moment you're ready, you give me the word."

She lifts her head and studies my face, hope blooming on hers. "Really?"

I cup her cheek, unable to stop smiling. Every time I look at her, I can't stop smiling. She's my girl and I love her more with every beat of my heart. "You want to start trying today, you just say the word."

"Well, remember last month before the wedding? Everything got really crazy and I got sick with tonsillitis and the doctor gave me an antibiotic?"

I nod. She was pretty sick for a few days there. But as soon as she was feeling good, she was all over me again. Hell, we were all over each other even though she hadn't finished the antibiotic quite yet.

"Well, um, turns out that you're supposed to use a backup method, or the antibiotic cancels out the pill. I didn't know that. Kind of wish Zoey had told me that one sooner." She chews on her lower lip.

I freeze on the spot. I can barely drag in a breath. "You're saying there's a chance you're pregnant?"

"I'm saying I am pregnant. Surprise?" She's so cute, all nervous about what I'm going to think. I've made no secret of the fact that I want a family. But we've always talked as if it were years off.

"That's a great surprise," I reassure her quickly and press a kiss to her forehead. "I want to breed you as often as I can."

She chuckles, all the tension fading from her body as she snuggles back into my arms. "Let's just start with one for now."

I rub her back in a slow, soothing circle the way she likes. "Never be nervous about being pregnant.

Any babies we're lucky enough to have will always be a blessing."

"Even if we have a dozen?" She teases.

"Especially then," I promise. I still don't know how I got so lucky as to have this beautiful woman. She always supports my ideas and loves me unconditionally. With her by my side, I feel as if I can conquer the world and now, we're starting a family together. It doesn't get better than that.

Want a bonus scene with Piper and Gray? Sign up for my weekly newsletter and get the bonus scene here.

Psst…want to see Brock and Zoey fall in love after she accidentally moons him? You can read **Romancing the Sheriff** today!

MOUNTAIN MEN DO IT BETTER

Everyone knows that mountain men do it better. Skip the hike and grab your kindle to head up to the mountains this fall in this fun, swoon-worthy series!

Rescued by the Mountain Man by Mia Brody
Taken by the Mountain Man by Kaci Rose
Roughing It With the Mountain Man by Frankie Love
Tempted by the Mountain Man by Rebecca Wilder

TEASER: ROMANCING THE SHERIFF

I glance at the odometer and my heart sinks. We still have another ten miles up the road before I arrive at the lodge. The miles are crawling by since I'm inching up the mountain. Even with the promised snow tires, I don't feel comfortable driving in this winter wonderland.

When he whines again, I look in the rearview mirror. "Do you have to go as bad as I do?"

It's not like the mountain has rest stops or gas stations on it. No, the beautiful remote location means we're on our own until we make it up to our cabin. Except I don't think I can wait that long. The extra-large hot chocolate was too much for me.

"Alright, if you promise that we won't fall off the mountain, we can stop," I tell him.

Woofer sighs in relief as I navigate the car to a spot on the side of the road. If we walk into the clearing a little bit, no one should be able to see us even if they do happen to drive along. Not that I expect another car to come through here. There isn't a lot of traffic on the mountain.

I let my little dog do his business before I wrap his leash around the branch of one of the barren trees. That's when I realize my predicament. The snowy landscape means there are no leaves or brush visible, nothing to dry off with afterwards.

Glancing at the tree, I see there's a fine covering of a brown vine over the trunk and branches. Little white berries are clumped together on the hairy plant. The vine isn't the ideal solution, but it's going to have to do.

The wind howls as I do my business, and I have to work to stay balanced despite my wide hips and curvy figure. I've been camping before when I was younger. But I always had access to an outhouse at least. Here, I'm exposed to the elements.

"This feels like the opening to one of those urban legends where the girl disappears mysteriously," I tell Woofer.

He cocks his head, the way he does when I'm telling him the details of one of my romance books.

He's a great listener. I've often joked with my friends that Woofer is the best boyfriend a girl could ask for. He's loyal, patient, and always listens to me.

He lets out a bark and stares intently into a patch of nearby trees.

"Don't you spook me like this," I hiss at my dog.

The hair on the back of my neck stands up as every creepy horror movie I've ever seen goes through my head. *The call was coming from inside the house.*

"You know what? We're going to sing a song," I say. It's what my Nana who raised me taught me to do any time I became scared or overwhelmed. By the time I'm halfway through the chorus, I'm starting to feel less frightened.

I reach for the hairy vine, still singing. I've just grazed it with my mitten when a loud, masculine voice yells, "Freeze."

I stop, my ass in the air and my heart pounding. Serial killers aren't supposed to announce themselves, are they? Is that against the rules in a horror movie? I can't remember.

"Whatever you do, don't touch that vine again."

I'm supposed to say something sassy and brave. I should show the viewers that I'm a plucky heroine they can root for, not the dumb redhead that goes down into the creepy basement and deserves to be bludgeoned. "Stop spying on me, you pervert!"

Gathering my courage, I glance over my shoulder. I should look him in the eye and assert dominance. Does that work on mountain perverts?

Suddenly, I'm staring into the bluest eyes I've ever seen. They're the exact shade of the Atlantic right after a storm has rolled in. His dark hair is tousled, and his thick beard has me remembering the way that Hugh Jackman in Wolverine makes my panties go wet.

He's wearing a uniform that identifies him as the local sheriff. Suddenly, I realize that this is easily the hottest man I've ever seen in real life and I'm squatting here with my pants around my ankles.

Read Romancing the Sheriff Now

Welcome to Courage County where protective alpha heroes fall for strong curvy women they love and defend. There's NO cheating and NO cliffhangers. Just a sweet, sexy HEA in each book.

Love on the Ranch

Her Alpha Cowboy

Pregnant and alone, Riley has nowhere to go until the alpha cowboy finds her. Will she fall in love with her rescuer?

Her Older Cowboy

Summer is making a baby with her brother's best friend. But he insists on making it the old-fashioned way.

Her Protector Cowboy

Jack will do whatever it takes to protect his curvy woman after their hot one-night stand...then he plans to claim her!

Her Forever Cowboy

Dean is in love with his best friend's widow. When they're stranded together for the night, will he finally tell her how he feels?

Her Dirty Cowboy

The ranch's newest hire also happens to be the woman Adam had a one-night stand with...and she's carrying his baby!

Her Sexy Cowboy

She's a scared runaway with a baby. He's determined to protect them both. But neither of them expected to fall in love.

Her Wild Cowboy

He'll keep his curvy woman safe, even if it means a marriage in name only. But what happens when he wants to make it a real marriage?

Her Wicked Cowboy

One hot night with Jake gave me the best gift of my life: a beautiful baby girl. Will he want us to be a family when I show up on his doorstep a year later?

Courage County Brides

The Cowboy's Bride

The only way out of my horrible life is to become a mail order bride. But will my new cowboy husband be willing to take a chance on love?

The Cowboy's Soulmate

Can a jaded playboy find forever with his curvy mail order bride and her baby? Or will her secret ruin their future?

The Cowboy's Valentine

I'm a grumpy loner cowboy and I like it that way. Until my beautiful mail order bride arrives and suddenly, I want more than a marriage in name only.

The Cowboy's Match

Will this mail order bride matchmaker take a chance on love when she falls for the bearded cowboy who happens to be her VIP client?

The Cowboy's Obsession

Can this stalker cowboy show the curvy schoolteacher that he's the one for her?

The Cowboy's Sweetheart

Rule #1 of becoming a mail order bride: never fall in love with your cowboy groom.

The Cowboy's Angel

Can this cowboy single dad with a baby find love with his new mail order bride?

The Cowboy's Heiress

This innocent heiress is posing as a mail order bride. But what happens when her grumpy cowboy husband discovers who she really is?

Courage County Warriors

Rescue Me

Getting out was hard. Knowing who to trust was easy: my dad's best friend. He's the only man I can count on, but will we be able to keep our hands off each other?

Protect Me

When I need a warrior to protect me, I know just who to turn to: my brother's best friend. But will this grumpy cowboy who's guarding my body break my heart?

Shield Me

When trouble comes for me, I know who to call—my ex-boyfriend's dad. He's the only one who can help. But can I convince this grumpy cowboy to finally claim me?

Courage County Fire & Rescue

The Firefighter's Curvy Nanny

As a single dad firefighter, I was only looking for a quick fling. Then the curvy woman from last night shows up. Turns out, she's my new nanny.

The Firefighter's Secret Baby

After a scorching one-night stand with a sexy firefighter, I realize I'm pregnant…with my brother's best friend's baby.

The Firefighter's Forbidden Fling

I knew a one night stand with my grumpy boss wasn't the best idea…but I didn't think it would lead to anything serious. I definitely didn't think it would lead to a surprise pregnancy with this sexy firefighter.

GET A FREE COWBOY ROMANCE

Get Her Grumpy Cowboy for FREE:
https://www.MiaBrody.com/free-cowboy/

LIKE THIS STORY?

If you enjoyed this story, please post a review about it. Share what you liked or didn't like. It may not seem like much, but reviews are so important for indie authors like me who don't have the backing of a big publishing house.

Of course, you can also share your thoughts with me via email if you'd prefer to reach out that way. My email address is mia @ miabrody.com (remove the spaces). I love hearing from my readers!

ABOUT THE AUTHOR

Mia Brody writes steamy stories about alpha men who fall in love with big, beautiful women. She loves happy endings and every couple she writes will get one!

When she's not writing, Mia is searching for the perfect slice of cheesecake and reading books by her favorite instalove authors.

Keep in touch when you sign up for her newsletter: https://www.MiaBrody.com/news. It's the fastest way to hear about her new releases so you never miss one!

Printed in Great Britain
by Amazon

61970380R00068